Some hamsters are timid little creatures, frightened of their own shadows, but not Hannibal! When chance throws him headlong into the strange and dangerous world outside his cage, he welcomes the opportunity to explore. The terrifyingly narrow escape from Owl, the friendly advice of Rabbit, the dire warning from Seagull he takes in his stride, learning as he goes along which creatures to trust and which to fear. But at the end of each adventure he is glad when rescue comes and he can return to the comfort and safety of his own home.

Hannibal
on the farm

Story by Raymond Howe
Illustrations by John Berry

Ladybird Books Ltd
Loughborough
1976

Hannibal the hamster was just settling down for a good day's sleep when the letter arrived. He heard it fall with a little 'bump' on the front door mat. He was suddenly wide awake. He just HAD to know what news the letter contained.

He did not have to wait long. Father opened the letter at breakfast time.

"It's from Uncle Charlie," said Father. "Uncle Charlie asks whether we can look after his farm for a few days whilst he has a holiday. He will be busy with the harvest next month; so if he doesn't take a holiday now, it will be too late."

"Oh! Yes!" said Elizabeth. "Please write back and say we can. It will be fun looking after all the animals."

"Looking after animals has to be done properly," said Father. "But if John will help, and Mother thinks she can look after us, we will go. Uncle Charlie deserves a holiday."

"I will help," said John.

"Good boy," said Father. "I knew we could rely upon you."

"I shall need some help, too," said Mother. "There is always something to do when you are managing a farmhouse – perhaps Elizabeth will help me?"

"Yes, Mother – I will do everything I can to help," said Elizabeth.

"We have to decide what to do about Hannibal," said Father.

"Oh, don't worry about Hannibal," answered Mother. "He will be perfectly happy to come with us. Looking after one more small animal will hardly make any difference at all."

"Good," said Father. "I'm glad that we can go. It is not easy, being responsible for a farm. But it is very worthwhile."

Very soon, everything was arranged. Father wrote a letter to Uncle Charlie saying that the family would arrive at the farm on the next Saturday morning.

Saturday came at last, and Hannibal's cage was placed on the back seat of the car. Hannibal had travelled with the family many times before, and he was quite unconcerned; he simply curled up inside his cosy bed and fell asleep.

He was just waking up again when the family arrived at the farm. He stretched his paws, and yawned, and twitched his whiskers, wondering in rather lazy fashion what life on a farm would be like. A bit dull, perhaps? Not very exciting for a hamster?

The car door slammed.

"Give Hannibal to me," said Mother. "I'll take him into the house."

Hannibal felt his cage go swinging through the air. But somehow Elizabeth did not hand it over properly, and Mother missed the handle.

The cage fell down with a crash. Hannibal was shaken out of his cosy nest. The whole of one side of the cage sprang away as it struck the cobbled stones of the farmyard.

Hannibal was very frightened. His first instinct was to run and hide. He scampered away towards the nearest shelter.

It happened that there was a field of wheat very near to the farmhouse. The stalks had grown tall, and the ears of corn were ripening in the sun.

Hannibal ran deep into the tall wheat. In a little while he had quite forgotten his fear. He was soon rambling along quite happily in one of the long hollows which ran through the field. He came to a place where some wheat had been beaten flat by the rain. He nibbled at some of the grain. It was not quite ripe, and it had a milky taste which Hannibal found quite delicious. He stuffed his cheek-pouches with the grain until they bulged out to twice their normal size; then he went back among the tall stalks to find a place to sleep.

When Hannibal woke up, it was evening. The sun had not set, and the earth where he lay was warm. For some moments he did not move, then he sniffed the fresh air happily and began to look around him.

He listened to the wind; it made a whispering sound as it rustled among the ears of wheat.

Then Hannibal realised that there was something else whispering besides the wind. It was the voice of a small creature, and it was coming from above.

Hannibal looked up. High among the tall stalks, the voice said, "Hello – I'm Harvest Mouse. This is my home."

Harvest Mouse was the smallest animal Hannibal had ever met. She seemed to be hanging in the air but in fact she was half way up one of the tall wheat-stalks. Her tail was wrapped round and round the ripening straw, and she seemed to be quite comfortable.

"Hello," said Hannibal. "I hope I didn't frighten you."

"Oh, no," said Harvest Mouse. "I thought you were really quite harmless – you've been asleep for most of the day."

"Yes," said Hannibal. "Hamsters always sleep in the daytime, and wake up at night."

"It is very dangerous to travel at night," said Harvest Mouse. "There are many hunters in the fields at night."

"I will be careful," said Hannibal.

"You are safe in the tall wheat," said Harvest Mouse. "Large animals cannot move through it without making a noise, and Owl cannot see clearly when the ears are constantly moving in the wind. Although I am tiny and helpless, I can live here quite safely. I build my nest high above the ground."

It was true. Harvest Mouse had built her nest among the tall stems. It was very small – not really much bigger than Hannibal himself – and it was perfectly round. Harvest Mouse had plaited the grassy nest very carefully between several wheat-stems.

"What a beautiful nest!" exclaimed Hannibal.

"Yes – I have eight babies in there," said Harvest Mouse. "There's hardly room for me!"

"Do you know what lies beyond the wheatfield?" asked Hannibal.

"No – I cannot help you," said Harvest Mouse. "Many of my kind are carried to the barns at harvest time, and few find their way back. But I was lucky. I escaped when the wheat fell, and I burrowed into the earth, and there I spent the winter. The wheatfield is the whole world, for me and my kind."

"I must find my way back to the farm," said Hannibal. "Thank you for being so friendly. Goodbye."

Hannibal turned back the way he had come. It was quite easy for him to run back along the hollow in the earth; he found that it was not as far as he had thought. He soon came to the edge of the wheatfield.

As he broke out from between the tall stalks, he almost bumped into Gosling. Gosling had a long neck, big flat feet and a yellow beak. He had his head down, and his beak was snuffling through the loose earth, searching the edge of the field for stray grains of wheat. He sprang back with a great squawk as Hannibal appeared.

"Oh! Oh! Dear me! Are you Fox?" he cried. "Don't come any closer! My mother is only just round the corner."

"I'm not Fox," said Hannibal quickly. "I'm Hannibal the hamster."

"That's all right, then," said Gosling. He sounded very relieved.

"Who is Fox?" asked Hannibal.

"I have never seen him," said Gosling. "But Mother says he is a dreadful creature. Fox comes in the night, and carries goslings like me away to his den. The only safe place is within the wire. My mother's house is inside the wire enclosure, but I wanted to eat the grain from the wheatfield. Mother said I should be quite safe until dark."

"I need to find a safe place," said Hannibal. "May I come inside the wire?"

"Of course," said Gosling.

Gosling lived in a little wooden house which stood at the top of a small hill. The house had no windows; but there was an opening in the front big enough to allow Gosling and his mother to pass in and out. There was a pile of warm straw inside.

"I shall be safe here," said Hannibal. "Thank you."

Mother Goose stood in the hollow with all the other grown-up geese. Her feet were very muddy.

The hollow was made by a tiny stream, and the geese were very happy, sloshing in the mud all day.

By now the light was beginning to fade. The cows were wandering back to the meadow after being milked. They were black and white cows, and they walked in single file.

After the cows had passed by, John appeared.
He was carrying a bucket of grain. He threw
several handfuls from the bucket into the goose pen.
The geese ate a very noisy supper, and then
waddled into the little wooden house to sleep.
Hannibal curled up in the straw, twitched his
whiskers once, and closed his eyes.

Later in the night, Hannibal woke up. A bright moon was shining. He crept out of the little house and made his way to the wire wall of the goose pen. He was just about to squeeze through when he saw Fox.

Hannibal crouched down in the grass. He hardly dared look beyond the wire.

Fox was striding round the fence, looking very carefully for a gap in the wire. His coat glowed dark red in the moonlight. His great tail flowed behind him. His ears were pointed and very alert.

As Fox came to the place where Hannibal was hiding, Sheepdog began to bark.

Fox was startled. He drew back from the wire. Then he ran swiftly away. The white tip of his tail dipped and disappeared. Fox was gone.

Sheepdog came hurrying to the goose pen.

"It was fortunate that you were inside the wire," he said to Hannibal. "Fox is very dangerous."

"Yes," said Hannibal. "But he is very beautiful, too!"

Sheepdog sank down on his haunches into the grass. He looked rather like Fox in some ways, although his coat was black and white and his ears were floppy. He had a very handsome tail.

"I keep an eye on the geese at night," he said. "But my real work is with the sheep."

"What are sheep?" asked Hannibal.

"Sheep are large woolly creatures," said Sheepdog. "I suppose they're really rather stupid, too. We keep them all together, in a flock."

Sheepdog suddenly opened his mouth wide, showing off his perfect teeth.

"I'm having a quiet time just now," he said. "The lambs are growing up, and we have finished shearing for this year."

"What is shearing?" asked Hannibal.

"Shearing means taking the wool from the sheep," said Sheepdog. "It is done in the summer. I have to work with Shepherd. We work very well together – perhaps this is because we always understand each other perfectly."

Sheepdog paused. He seemed to be very proud of his work.

"When Shepherd wants one particular sheep, he sends me into the flock," said Sheepdog. "Then with a snap! snap! round I go; I cut it out, away from the crowd, and bring it back to Shepherd. I can get any of them. Whichever one that Shepherd wants."

"Do you hurt it?" asked Hannibal.

"Goodness, no!" said Sheepdog. "Sheep are valuable. I guard them. I care for them just as much as Shepherd does."

"How very interesting," said Hannibal politely.

Sheepdog rose and shook his coat. "I must go now," he said. "Strangers are looking after the farm. They may need my help."

"Goodbye," said Hannibal.

The farmyard was very quiet when Sheepdog had gone. Hannibal decided to try to find his way back to the house. He set off.

Morning was not far away. The sky was beginning to light up in the east. One by one the stars faded. Hannibal was half way across the yard when Rooster crowed.

"Goodness! How you frightened me!" cried Hannibal.

"I am sorry," said Rooster. "I must crow when morning comes. Who would not crow when the sun returns? Each new day fills me with such joy and wonder that I must stand up and crow as loudly as I can." Rooster lifted his head and crowed again. "How wonderful the morning is!" he said. He turned his proud head, and the feathers on his neck glowed red and gold in the first light of day.

The sun rose, and the farm buildings cast deep black shadows on the ground. "All our barns are empty now," said Rooster. "They will soon be full of the wheat and oats and barley that the sun has ripened. Harvest is very near."

Hannibal looked up at the high walls of the barns. He felt happier now that he was near to the farmhouse. "Does anyone live in the barns?" he asked.

"Tabby lives there," said Rooster at once. "He hunts the rats who would steal our grain if they could."

"Who is Tabby?" asked Hannibal.

"Tabby is the farm cat," said Rooster. "Take good care that he does not find you. If you have to cross the open yard, it would be better for you to wait until night comes again."

"May I stay under your house?" asked Hannibal

"You are very welcome," said Rooster. "No one will disturb you. I am master here. No hen questions my rule; dogs and cats respect me." Rooster crowed again. "Before you sleep, remember this," he said. "Tabby always has a saucer of milk just after darkness falls. It will be safe for you to cross the yard then."

"Thank you," said Hannibal. "Goodbye."

He dug himself into the warm earth under the chicken house, twitched his whiskers once, and fell asleep.

Hannibal woke up once during the day. The engine of the farm wagon roared. Hannibal sleepily watched it as it turned and went out of the gate towards the road. Then he dozed off again.

When it was dark, Hannibal crawled out of his hiding place. He listened. The farmyard was very quiet. He could see a light in the window of the farmhouse. He made his way cautiously out into the open yard, and ran towards the farmhouse door. Where was Tabby? he wondered.

He had almost reached the farmhouse door when the great white light fell upon him. The farm wagon had returned. The light which it carried in front of it filled the whole sky with a glaring brilliance. Hannibal couldn't move. He seemed to be pinned down to the ground where he stood. The roar of the wagon's engine deafened him. He did not hear the sound of the wagon's door as it opened.

The shadow of Tabby moved at the edge of the
great white light. But the farm cat was afraid of its
glare, and he hesitated. Just as he was about to
pounce on Hannibal, a massive black shadow
blotted out the light.

Then a man's voice said, "No, Tabby!
Go away!"

The man's hand descended and scooped
Hannibal up. He passed safely through the
farmhouse door.

"Guess what I've found," said Father.

"Hannibal!" cried Elizabeth, as Father opened his hand.

"Where *have* you been?" said Mother.

"We shall never know," said Father. "What I do know is that I spotted him in the headlamps of the wagon as I turned into the gate. Poor Hannibal – he was too terrified to move."

Hannibal was soon back in his familiar cage. His bed was wonderfully soft, and he found one or two hazel nuts in his food store. He stuffed them into his cheek-pouches just for the sheer pleasure of feeling them there. It was so good to be back.

In a day or two, Uncle Charlie returned. He looked round the farm, and he seemed very pleased with all that the family had done. "You have looked after everything very well," he said.

"Yes," said Father. "We didn't lose anything – except Hannibal!"

Everyone laughed.

Very soon it was time to return home. Elizabeth was very careful when she loaded the hamster's cage into the car. Hannibal thought of Harvest Mouse, and wondered what would happen to her when the wheat was cut down. He thought of Fox, and remembered how beautiful he was.

Hannibal thought about all the important work that Sheepdog did on the farm, and of how lucky he had been to have met such an animal. And then Hannibal remembered that he had come to the farm himself, expecting to have a dull time! Well, it had not been dull, after all. It had been very exciting indeed.

In fact, everything had been so exciting that it was really too much for one tiny hamster. Hannibal felt suddenly very glad that he was on his way home again. He was quite worn out.

He yawned, twitched his whiskers once, and fell fast asleep.